This
Treasure Cove Story
belongs to

_____

TANGLED

A CENTUM BOOK 978-1-912841-12-7
Published in Great Britain by Centum Books Ltd.
This edition published 2019.

3 5 7 9 10 8 6 4 2

Centum Books Ltd, 20 Devon Square, Newton Abbot,
Devon, TQ12 2HR, UK.

www.centumbooksltd.co.uk | books@centumbooksltd.co.uk
CENTUM BOOKS Limited Reg. No. 07641486.

A CIP catalogue record for this book is available
from the British Library.

Printed in China.

centum

FSC
www.fsc.org

MIX
Paper from
responsible sources
FSC® C149078

A Treasure Cove Story

Disney PRINCESS

Tangled

Adapted by
Ben Smiley

Illustrated by
Victoria Ying

Rapunzel had long, long hair and lived in a tall, tall tower. Her hair was as long as the tower was tall. When Mother Gothel came home every day, she called, '**Rapunzel, let down your hair!**' And Rapunzel pulled Mother Gothel up into the tower.

Rapunzel's hair was **magical**. It kept Mother Gothel young and beautiful.

Rapunzel did not know that Mother Gothel had stolen her from her real parents, the King and the Queen.

Mother Gothel wanted the **magical** hair all for herself.

Mother Gothel never let Rapunzel leave the tower. She told Rapunzel that bad people wanted to take her **magical** hair. Rapunzel had one friend — a chameleon named **Pascal**.

Once a year, on her birthday, Rapunzel saw **sparkling lights** floating into the sky. She wished she could leave the tower and see the lights up close. They seemed **meant** for her.

One day, just before Rapunzel's eighteenth birthday, a thief named **Flynn** was running through the forest. He had stolen the lost princess's crown. While trying to get away from Maximus, a determined horse from the royal guard, Flynn found Rapunzel's hidden tower.

Flynn climbed up the tower to hide. Rapunzel had never seen another person besides Mother Gothel. Rapunzel thought Flynn wanted her hair. But he didn't. Rapunzel showed Flynn a painting she had made of the **lights** and asked him to take her to see them. Flynn agreed.

On the way, Flynn and Rapunzel stopped in a pub. It was filled with scary-looking men. But they didn't want to steal Rapunzel's hair, either. They were **friendly**.

Maximus and some royal guards found Flynn. One of the scary-looking men helped Flynn and Rapunzel escape.

They ran until they got trapped in a water-filled cave. Rapunzel's magical **glowing** hair helped them find a way out!

But Maximus found Flynn again. The horse wanted to take Flynn to jail. Rapunzel told **Maximus** it was her birthday. She asked him to let Flynn take her to see the sparkling lights. Maximus agreed. Rapunzel's wish was about to come true!

Flynn and Rapunzel had a **wonderful** day. A little boy gave Rapunzel a small kingdom flag. The kingdom was celebrating the birthday of the lost princess.

The lost princess had the same birthday as Rapunzel!

Rapunzel saw a picture of the King and the Queen holding their baby princess. The Queen and the Princess had **green eyes** — just like Rapunzel!

Suddenly, Rapunzel was swept up in a dance! It was the most **fun** she had ever had... so far.

That night, the people of the kingdom lit lanterns.
At last, Rapunzel's wish came true. Overjoyed, she saw the
sparkling lights fill the sky. She loved the world outside
the tower. She loved Flynn. And he loved her, too.

On shore, Flynn left Rapunzel and did not return. Rapunzel was **heartbroken**. She did not know that Flynn had been tricked by evil Mother Gothel. He had been captured and put in jail! Mother Gothel found Rapunzel and took her back to the tower.

Back in her room, Rapunzel realized that she had been painting the kingdom's emblem, the **golden sun**, on her wall her entire life!

Rapunzel remembered the picture of the **lost princess** and the Queen. Now Rapunzel knew why they all looked alike.

Mother Gothel was the only one who wanted to steal Rapunzel's **magical** hair. She had lied to Rapunzel about everything. '**Mother, I am the lost princess!**' Rapunzel said.

Meanwhile, Flynn had escaped and arrived at the tower to rescue Rapunzel.

'Rapunzel! Rapunzel! Let down your hair!' he called.

But Mother Gothel would not let Rapunzel go. Mother Gothel hurt Flynn so badly that he could never, ever take Rapunzel from her.

Flynn still thought of a way to save Rapunzel. He **cut** her hair. Without Rapunzel's magical hair, Mother Gothel withered away. Rapunzel was finally free of the evil woman.

But without her long hair, Rapunzel had no more magic
to save Flynn. He closed his eyes for the last time.

Rapunzel cried. A single **golden tear** fell on Flynn's cheek.
It contained the last bit of magic left inside Rapunzel. Flynn's
eyes opened! He was all right!

Rapunzel went to her real parents, the King and the Queen. After eighteen years of waiting, they took one look at the **green-eyed** girl and knew she was their daughter. Rapunzel had come home at last!

Rapunzel loved her new life. She loved the world outside the tower. She loved her new friends. At last, she knew where she belonged.

And they all lived **happily** ever after.

Treasure Cove Stories

Please contact Centum Books to receive the full list of titles in the *Treasure Cove Stories* series. books@centumbooksltd.co.uk

1 Three Little Pigs
2 Snow White and the Seven Dwarfs
3 The Fox and the Hound - Hide-and-Seek
4 Dumbo
5 Cinderella
6 Cinderella's Friends
7 Alice in Wonderland
8 Mad Hatter's Tea Party from Alice in Wonderland
9 Mickey Mouse and his Spaceship
10 Peter Pan
11 Pinocchio
12 Mickey and the Beanstalk
13 Sleeping Beauty and the Good Fairies
14 The Lucky Puppy
15 Chicken Little
16 The Incredibles
17 Coco
18 Winnie the Pooh and Tigger
19 The Sword in the Stone
20 Mary Poppins
21 The Jungle Book
22 Aristocats
23 Lady and the Tramp
24 Bambi
25 Bambi - Friends of the Forest
26 Pete's Dragon
27 Beauty and the Beast - The Teapot's Tale
28 Monsters, Inc. – M is for Monster
29 Finding Nemo
30 The Incredibles 2
31 The Incredibles – Jack-Jack Attack
33 Wall-E
34 Up
35 The Princess and the Frog
36 Toy Story – The Pet Problem

39 Spider-Man – Night of the Vulture!
40 Wreck it Ralph
41 Ralph Breaks the Internet
42 The Invincible Iron Man – Eye of the Dragon
45 Toy Story – A Roaring Adventure
46 Cars – Deputy Mater Saves the Day!
47 Spider-Man – Trapped by the Green Goblin
49 Spider-Man – High Voltage!
50 Frozen
51 Cinderella is my Babysitter
52 Beauty and the Beast - I am the Beast
56 I am a Princess
57 The Big Book of Paw Patrol
58 Paw Patrol - Adventures with Grandpa!
59 Paw Patrol - Pirate Pups!
60 Trolls
61 Trolls Holiday
63 Zootropolis
64 Ariel is my Babysitter
65 Tiana is my Babysitter
66 Belle is my Babysitter
67 Paw Patrol - Itty-Bitty Kitty Rescue
68 Moana
70 Guardians of the Galaxy
71 Captain America - High-Stakes Heist!
72 Ant-Man
73 The Mighty Avengers
74 The Mighty Avengers - Lights Out!
75 The Incredible Hulk
78 Paw Patrol - All-Star Pups!
80 I am Ariel
82 Jasmine is my Babysitter
87 Beauty and the Beast - I am Belle
88 The Lion Guard - The Imaginary Okapi
89 Thor - Thunder Strike!
90 Guardians of the Galaxy - Rocket to the Rescue!
93 Olaf's Frozen Adventure
95 Trolls - Branch's Bunker Birthday

96 Trolls - Poppy's Party
97 The Ugly Duckling
98 Cars - Look Out for Mater!
99 101 Dalmatians
100 The Sorcerer's Apprentice
101 Tangled
102 Avengers – The Threat of Thanos
105 The Mighty Thor
106 Doctor Strange
107 Captain Marvel
108 The Invincible Iron Man
110 The Big Freeze
111 Ratatouille
112 Aladdin
113 Aladdin - I am the Genie
114 Seven Dwarfs Find a House
115 Toy Story
116 Toy Story 4
117 Paw Patrol - Jurassic Bark!
118 Paw Patrol - Mighty Pup Power!
121 The Lion King - I am Simba
122 Winnie the Pooh - The Honey Tree
123 Frozen II
124 Baby Shark and the Colours of the Ocean
125 Baby Shark and the Police Sharks!
126 Trolls World Tour
127 I am Elsa
128 I am Anna
129 I am Olaf
130 I am Mulan
131 Sleeping Beauty
132 Onward
133 Paw Patrol – Puppy Birthday to You!
134 Black Widow
135 Trolls – Poppy's Big Day!
136 Baby Shark and the Tooth Fairy
137 Baby Shark – Mummy Shark
138 Inside Out
139 The Prince and the Pauper
140 Finding Dory
142 The Lion King - Simba's Daring Rescue

Book list may be subject to change. Not all titles are listed.